For
Emily and Daniel
M. W.

For
Joe and Sam
B. F.

First U. S. edition 2001

Library of Congress Cataloging-in-Publication Data

Waddell, Martin.
Tom Rabbit / Martin Waddell ; illustrated by Barbara Firth.—1st U.S. ed.
p. cm.
Summary: After spending an enjoyable day on the farm, Sammy and his toy rabbit become separated but happily find each other at bedtime.
ISBN 0-7636-1089-5
[1. Rabbits — Fiction. 2. Toys—Fiction.] I. Firth, Barbara, ill. II. Title.
PZ7.W1137 Tm 2001 [E] — dc21 99-088332

2 4 6 8 10 9 7 5 3

Printed in Italy

This book was typeset in Golden Cockerel.
The illustrations were done in pencil and watercolor.

Candlewick Press
2067 Massachusetts Avenue
Cambridge, Massachusetts 02140

visit us at www.candlewick.com

Tom Rabbit

Martin Waddell

illustrated by

Barbara Firth

CANDLEWICK PRESS
CAMBRIDGE, MASSACHUSETTS

One summer evening
Tom Rabbit and Sammy
went out to the back field
to see the real rabbits.

Tom Rabbit and Sammy
climbed up on the wall.

"We can see the whole world
from here," Sammy said
to Tom Rabbit.

"I'm happy with Sammy,"
Tom Rabbit thought.

Then Harry came by the back field with the cows, and Sammy ran off to help Harry.

Tom Rabbit was left all alone on the wall.

"Sammy won't be gone long," thought Tom Rabbit.

Mom called Sammy in
for his supper, and Sammy
went into the house.

"I hope Sammy comes back,"
thought Tom Rabbit.

The sun set on the field
and the moon rose.

"I've never seen that before,"
thought Tom Rabbit.

And then,
from the bank
at the end of the lane
the wild rabbits came . . .

first one
and then two
and then three
and then four
and then **more**.

Wild rabbits were there,

everywhere . . .

everywhere that
Tom Rabbit could see.

"I wish Sammy were here,"
thought Tom Rabbit.

A rabbit hopped up on the wall.
It quivered its nose
at Tom Rabbit.

"It's only a rabbit the same as
I am," thought Tom Rabbit.
"I'm not scared
one bit."

The light went on in Sammy's bedroom. Tom Rabbit saw it shine over the field.

"Sammy won't go to bed without me!" thought Tom Rabbit.

"Sammy can't go to bed without me," thought Tom Rabbit.

The light went out
in Sammy's bedroom.

"Sammy's gone to bed without
me," thought Tom Rabbit.
"I'm all alone now."

And that's when . . .

. . . Sammy came back
for Tom Rabbit.

"I'm sorry I left you,
Tom Rabbit," said Sammy,
and he carried Tom Rabbit
back home.

Tom Rabbit and Sammy
got into bed.

"Good night, Sammy,"
said Mom. "And good night,
Tom Rabbit."

"Good night, Mom,"
said Sammy.

"I'm happy with Sammy,"
Tom Rabbit thought,
and he snuggled down
safe in bed
beside Sammy.